WELCOME TO THE FAR NORTH... AND THE WORLD OF THE MICEKINGS!

WHERE THEY LIVE: Miceking Island

CAPITAL: Mouseborg, home of the Stiltonord family

OTHER VILLAGES: Oofadale, village of the Oofa Oofas, and Feargard, village of the vilekings

CLIMATE: Cold, cold, cold, especially when the icy north wind blows!

TYPICAL FOOD: Gloog, a superstinky but fabumouse stew. The secret recipe is closely guarded by the wife of the miceking chief.

NATIONAL DRINK: Finnbrew, made of equal parts codfish juice and herring juice, with a splash of squid ink

MEANS OF TRANSPORTATION: The drekar, a light but very fast ship

GREATEST HONOR: The miceking helmet. It is only earned when a mouse performs an act of courage or wins a Miceking Challenge.

UNIT OF MEASUREMENT: A mouseking tail (full tail, half tail, third tail, quarter tail)

ENEMIES: The terrible dragons who live in Beastgard

MEET THE STILTONORD FAMILY ...

GERONIMO
Advisor to the
miceking chief

THEA
A horse trainer who
works well with all kinds
of animals

TRAP
The most famouse
inventor in Mouseborg

BUGSILDA
Benjamin's best
friend

BENJAMIN
Geronimo's nephew

. . . AND THE EVIL DRAGONS!

The dragons are divided into 5 clans, all of which are terrifying!

1. Devourers
They love to eat micekings raw — no cooking necessary.

2. Steamers
They grab micekings, then fly over volcanoes so the steam and smoke make them taste good.

3. Biters
Before eating micekings, they nibble them delicately to see if they like them or not.

4. Slurpers
They wrap their long tongues around micekings and slurp them up.

5. Rinsers
As soon as they catch micekings, they rinse them in a stream to wash them off.

Geronimo Stilton

MICEKINGS

PULL THE DRAGON'S TOOTH!

Scholastic Inc.

Copyright © 2014 by Edizioni Piemme S.p.A., Palazzo Mondadori, Via Mondadori 1, 20090 Segrate, Italy. International Rights © Atlantyca S.p.A. English translation © 2016 by Atlantyca S.p.A.

The publisher does not have any control over and does not assume any responsibility for author or third-party websites or their content.

GERONIMO STILTON names, characters, and related indicia are copyright, trademark, and exclusive license of Atlantyca S.p.A. All rights reserved. The moral right of the author has been asserted. Based on an original idea by Elisabetta Dami. www.geronimostilton.com

Published by Scholastic Inc., *Publishers since 1920*, 557 Broadway, New York, NY 10012. SCHOLASTIC and associated logos are trademarks and/or registered trademarks of Scholastic Inc.

Stilton is the name of a famous English cheese. It is a registered trademark of the Stilton Cheese Makers' Association. For more information, go to www.stiltoncheese.com.

No part of this publication may be reproduced, stored in a retrieval system, or transmitted in any form or by any means, electronic, mechanical, photocopying, recording, or otherwise, without written permission of the copyright holder. For information regarding permission, please contact: Atlantyca S.p.A., Via Leopardi 8, 20123 Milan, Italy; e-mail foreignrights@atlantyca.it, www.atlantyca.com.

ISBN 978-1-338-03288-8

Text by Geronimo Stilton
Original title *Toglilo tu, il dente al dragante!*
Cover by Giuseppe Facciotto (pencils) and Flavio Ferron (ink and color)
Illustrations by Giuseppe Facciotto (pencils) and Alessandro Costa (ink and color)
Graphics by Chiara Cebraro

Special thanks to Tracey West
Translated by Julia Heim
Interior design by Kay Petronio

10 9 8 7 6 5 4 3 2 1   16 17 18 19 20

Printed in the U.S.A.   40
First printing 2016

WHAT'S THE BIG SECRET?

It was a calm **summer** evening in **Mouseborg**, the capital village of Miceking Island. The sun was setting over the mountains, and a *fresh breeze* blew across my fur. I whistled as I walked home.

Sorry, I haven't introduced myself. My name is *GERONIMO STILTONORD*, and I am a **MOUSEKING**!

As I walked, two young rodents **RACED** past me: my nephew Benjamin and his best friend, Bugsilda.

"It's so EXCITING!" said Benjamin.

"Yes, it's really EXCITING!" agreed Bugsilda.

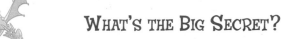
"What's so **EXCITING**?" I called out as they raced past.

"Oh, nothing," replied Benjamin, and they ran away, giggling.

HOW STRANGE!

Next I passed the hut of Copper Ironpaws, the village blacksmith.

"It's so EXCITING!" Copper was saying to another mouseking.

His customer glanced at me. "**Shh**, he's coming."

I marched up to them. "What's so exciting?"

"Oh, **NOTHING**," the mouse said quickly. "You must have heard wrong."

HOW VERY STRANGE!

What's exciting?

Oh, nothing.

Hee, hee!

I was almost at my hut when I saw a group of micekings talking very **quietly**. My cousin **Trap**, the village inventor, was among them.

"Careful, it's him!" I heard Trap whisper as I got near.

The micekings SCATTERED, chuckling.

HOW VERY, VERY STRANGE!

But . . .

HEE, HEE, HEE

"Trap, what is **HAPPENING**?" I asked. "Why is it that every time I show up somewhere, everyone stops talking and *giggles*?"

"I don't know what you mean, Cousin," Trap said. "There's nothing going on. Tee, hee!"

I was starting to become annoyed. "Fine! I don't care about your little secrets anyway!"

Then I stomped into my hut and settled in for what I hoped would be a relaxing night. I prepared a delicious pot of hot cheese soup and was about to dig in when someone **KNOCKED** on my door.

A Surprise for Me

My sister, **THEA**, was outside the door. "Geronimo, open up!" she called out.

"Have you come to laugh at me, too?" I **yelled** through the door. "I am tired of all these secrets!"

"Don't be a codfish," Thea said. "Open the door!"

"**NO, NO, NO!**"

I said stubbornly.

I am fed up!

I heard Thea sigh. "Oh, all right. But then I'll have to tell Sven that you **REFUSED** to come out of your hut. I warned you."

I jumped up. "Sven the Shouter wants me? Our village leader? Why didn't you say that before?"

I hurried to open the door. Thea entered and grabbed a hunk of **BreaD** from my table.

"Sven **ORDERED** us not to tell you anything so we wouldn't ruin the surprise," she explained.

My whiskers trembled with excitement. "A **SURPRISE?** For me? What is it? A new goatskin **blanket**? A precious **scroll**? A big chunk of Stenchberg **cheese**?" My mouth watered at the thought of it.

I was so **curious** I was practically jumping out of my fur!

Then we heard **noises** outside. "That must

be the others," Thea said.

"Others? What others?" I asked. "I'm not expecting anyone."

But Thea ignored me and opened the door. A **sea** of micekings invaded! They made themselves **COMFORTABLE** right away. They **sat** on my chairs. They **BOUNCED** on my bed. They **ATE** all

my bread and drank my cheese soup!

My humble home now held every rodent in Mouseborg!

"Great groaning glaciers!" I yelled. "What is everyone doing here?"

Right at that moment, Sven the Shouter stepped in. He **POUNDED** me on the back with his paw.

"I have gathered all the micekings here in your hut, you smarty-mouseking!" he thundered.

I nodded nervously.

"I need to make an **IMPORTANT** announcement!" Sven said. "MAX MUSCLEPAW, the great-great-great-grandson of the legendary Moki Musclepaw, has arrived in Mouseborg!"

I've got quite a surprise for you!

Ouch!

The micekings let out a **CHEER**.

"HOORAY FOR MAX MUSCLEPAW!

Hooray for the mouseking hero who has earned **1,753 MICEKING HELMETS**!"

Shivering squids! That's a lot of miceking helmets, the highest honor of the micekings!

"Is the **surprise** that Max is here?" I asked. "What does that have to do with me?"

Sven gave me a **PIERCING** stare. "It has **everything** to do with you, you shrimpsnout! I asked **MAX MUSCLEPAW** to come back to make YOU into a true macho mouseking!"

Is This the Little Shrimp I'm Supposed to Train?

Sven **LOOKED** me up and down, from the tips of my whiskers to the end of my **TAIL**. Then he frowned.

"A true macho mouseking needs muscles!" he barked. "You are as **SQUISHY** as a jellyfish!"

A glacial **chill** ran down my spine.

Sven continued. "So I have decided that you need a special trainer!"

"SO SAYS SVEN THE SHOUTER!"

the micekings cheered.

"Well said, oh fearless leader!" my cousin

12

Have you seen these muscles?

Trap chimed in.

I scowled at Trap, but he kept talking.

"Either you have muscles or you don't, and I have plenty," Trap said, flexing his meaty (but not very muscly) arm. "But you, Cousin, are as SOFT as a ball of mozzarella!"

"**WISE WORDS!**" Sven the Shouter agreed. "Trap, I order you to also participate in the special training so you can show Geronimo how a macho mouseking trains!"

Trap tried to protest. "Um, well, that wouldn't be **fair** to the other micekings, would it?" he asked.

"Yes, why can't we train, too?" the other micekings asked.

Taking advantage of the **CONFUSION**, I tried to quickly slip out of there. I was a whisker away from the exit, when . . . the door **SWUNG OPEN** and hit me right in the snout!

Helmets and herring, that hurt!

"Geronimo, where are you going?"

I looked up to see **THORA**, Sven's charming daughter!

"Well I . . . I j-just remembered I have something **important** to do!" I stuttered.

Then the door **SWUNG OPEN** (again!).

"Geronimo, let me introduce you to **MAX MUSCLEPAW**, the great miceking hero!" Thora said.

He's enormouse!

This is Max Musclepaw!

Hey there!

So there I stood, gazing up at the **tallest** and most **muscled** mouseking I had ever seen! He was as big as a block of **STONE** — no, as a **boulder** — no, as a whole **mountain**!

He looked me up and down.

"IS THIS THE LITTLE SHRIMP I'M SUPPOSED TO TRAIN?" he asked. "His tiny bones won't be crushed, will they?"

"Ha! A bit of **HARD WORK** never hurt anyone," boomed Sven. "And, to make everyone happy, I have decided that **CRUSHER**, **SMASHER**, and **SPRAINER** will participate in the training, too."

At those words, three **STRONG** micekings made their way through the crowd.

One by one they approached me, yelling:

You're Hopeless, You Smarty-Mouseking!

"**GET OUT OF BED**, shrimp!" Max Musclepaw yelled early the next morning as he dumped a bucket of **freezing** water on me.

"B-but, it's still **dark** outside!" I squeaked.

But this muscled hero didn't want to hear it. "A **TRUE MACHO MOUSEKING** gets up every day at dawn and starts to **RUN, RUN, RUN**!" he bellowed.

I reluctantly got out of bed, **yawning** like a bear just waking from hibernation. "Can't we at least have **breakfast**?" I asked.

Max gave me a **strange** smile. "Pack all

the food that you want in your bag. We will bring it with us to **Three Lookouts Cliff**."

SQUEAK! I was already hungry. I wanted to protest, but then I decided it was better to do what he said. (Have I mentioned that Max is very tall and **very muscled**?)

So I took the bag and stuffed it with:

✔ 22 eggs,
✔ **16** slices of **toast**,
✔ **20** jars of **FJORDBERRY JAM**,
✔ 25 logs of *goat cheese*, and
✔ **7** chunks of precious Stenchberg.

When I finished, the bag was

SO HEAVY!

"Lift that bag and run!" Max shouted.

"I WILL GET YOU IN SHAPE, YOU SMARTY-MOUSEKING!"

Crusher, Smasher, and Sprainer were waiting outside. The three of them had already begun their training, which consisted of:

100 **PUSH-UPS**,

100 **sit-ups**, and

100 **PULL-UPS** using their whiskers!

Guess what? **Trap** was nowhere in sight!

"Why don't you all start the trip without me?" I suggested. "I should wait here for my cousin."

"No need!" said Max. "Your cousin was so excited about the trip that he left early."

"**REALLY?**" I asked in disbelief.

"Yes, and you should follow his example, you **little shrimp**!" Max bellowed. "I'll

straighten you out, you smarty-mouseking!
Run, run, run!"

Then he began to chant:

"Our whiskers always make us proud!
We'll say it now! We'll say it loud!
And if the dragons we should meet,
We'll crush them in a fierce defeat!
We work, we stink, we sweat, we spit!
But we will never, ever quit!
Our enemies will feel our sting!
We are the true and mighty micekings!"

We ran through the village and began to
CLIMB up, up, up, all the way to Three
Lookouts Cliff. CRUSHER, SMASHER,
and **SPRAINER** ran behind me, shouting
all the way.

"Run or I'll **CRUSH** you!"

"Run or I'll SMASH you!"

"Run or I'll **SPRAIN** your tail!"

The hill we were climbing was so steep that the weight of my bag caused me to FALL backward, like a turtle in his shell.

How do I get into these terrible situations?

THREE LOOKOUTS CLIFF

We finally reached the top of **Three Lookouts Cliff**.

Max Musclepaw was there already. "You call that running?" he scoffed.

But I was tired — finished — exhausted!

I was also starving, so I opened my backpack.

"What are you doing, you **little shrimp**?" Max yelled at me.

"I—I was just preparing BREAKFAST, oh brave one," I replied hopefully.

He snickered. "I said you could **bring** breakfast. I didn't say you could eat it!"

I was puzzled, until Max said, "The breakfast is for the lookouts!"

"B-but . . . but . . ." I stammered.

"**Move it, shrimp!**" Max yelled.

He pushed me toward the **watchtower**, where three lookouts were scanning the horizon.

The lookouts stay in the tower DAY and NIGHT. They watch the sky for dragons, who

The Three Lookouts

These three micekings never leave the watchtower. They sound a large horn as a warning when dragons or other enemies are in sight.

are always starved for miceking meat!

I handed the lookouts my backpack **FULL** of food.

"Young mickings just aren't the same these days," grumbled the first.

"Since when did mickings becomes such **jellyfish**?" grumbled the second.

"This one looks as SOFT as a cheese ball," grumbled the third.

I sighed. Would I ever fit in?

Suddenly, Trap ran up to me. He looked sweaty and **STICKY** but seemed to be full of energy.

"Good morning, Cousin," he said cheerfully. "A nice little run is a great way to start the day!"

It was strange that Trap wasn't **exhausted** like I was. Even stranger, I thought I smelled **honey** on him.

Are you tired already?

Puff ... pant ...

"It's time to start our first exercise!" Max called out. "You need to **CRUSH** those rocks!"

I looked at the rocks. They were **giant boulders**!

Crusher, Smasher, and Sprainer started pounding the boulders, **crumbling** them with their bare paws.

"Snap to it, smarty-mouseking!" Max yelled at me.

I tried to picked up the **MALLET**, but it weighed as much as I did!

1 When I finally managed to lift it, I charged at the boulder, yelling, "Here I goooo!"

2 But I missed it and face-planted into the rock!

KABAAAAAAAAM!

Here I go!

2

Oops!

1

3 The **MALLET** slipped out of my paw, flew through the air, and landed right behind a GOAT that was munching on some grass nearby.

4 The goat, FURIOUS, charged at me with its head down! **SQUEAK!**

THE GREAT CLIFF DIVE

I closed my **EYES** and prepared for the worst as the goat **charged** toward me.

At the last second, Max Musclepaw grabbed the goat by its horns and stopped it in its tracks.

"YOU'D BE TOAST IF IT WEREN'T FOR ME, YOU LITTLE SHRIMP!"

he said.

He let go of the goat's horns. The animal trotted away, angrily *huffing* and *puffing*. The three lookouts had watched the whole scene from the watchtower.

"In our day . . ." began the first one.

"We respected goats!" said the **second** one.

"We certainly didn't throw mallets at them!" finished the **THIRD** one.

Shivering squids, I can't win!

Then Max gathered us together for our next exercise . . . *the great cliff dive.*

I looked over the edge and got woozy. What a **DIZZYING DROP** down to the water below!

"I'm afraid of heights!" I whimpered. "And I'm a terrible swimmer!"

At that moment, I felt a **STICKY** paw on my shoulder. It was Trap.

"Come on, Cousin!" he said. "Follow my lead. I'm not **afraid** of anything!"

Max Musclepaw stomped up to us, sniffing. "I smell **HONEY**." He GRABBED Trap by the belt. "It's you! You rubbed honey all over your fur to make yourself look **sweaty**. You didn't really run, did you?"

"Um . . . well . . . I took a **SHORTCUT**," Trap admitted.

"Is that so?" Max growled. "Then you can **JUMP** first! And don't try to **trick** me again!"

Max pushed Trap off the cliff! Then Crusher, Smasher, and Sprainer each **JUMPED** off. They all splashed into the **freezing** waters of the fjord.

I **LOOKED** down, turning as **pale**

You first!

as mozzarella, then as **purple** as a wild berry, then as **green** as the mold on Stenchberg cheese. Galloping goats, I'd never make it!

Max tried to encourage me. "Watch me!" he yelled.

As he dove off the cliff, he yelled, "**Get a move on, you little shriiiiiiiiiiiiiiimp!**"

The **THREE LOOKOUTS** approached me.

"To get over a fear of heights, you just need to hold your **BREATH**," said the first.

I'm scared!

"No, he needs to eat some snails," said the second.

"No way! He just needs to stick **pinecones** in his ears," said the third.

Then the first lookout sounded the horn right in my ear.

TOOOOOOOT!!

TOOOOOOOOOOOOOT!

I was so startled I jumped right off the cliff! I fell **DOWN**, **DOWN**, **DOWN** . . .

SEASICK AND HEARTBROKEN!

I made a mousetastic **dive** (well, more like a **BELLY FLOP**) and splashed into the waters of the fjord.

I can't swim, so Max FISHED me out of the water with a long oar. He pulled me up onto the deck of a drekar — a miceking ship.

"Stop splashing around, shrimp!" Max yelled. "Our captain is waiting!"

Captain? My whiskers **twitched**. I hoped it wasn't . . .

"*GERONIMO!* Hurry up and get on board. We need to leave while the wind is still in our favor," barked OLAF THE FEARLESS.

Hurry up!

We're leaving!

NOOOOOOOOOO!

Olaf was captain of the *Bated Breath*, the creakiest ship on all of Miceking Island! My tummy started to do **flip-flops** as waves rocked the ship. Then I saw **dark clouds** forming overhead.

squeak! A storm was coming!

"Don't worry, Geronimo. A **TRUE MACHO MOUSEKING** goes out to sea no matter what the weather!" Olaf said.

I sighed and sat down on the rower's bench.

Then I heard a voice from the shore.

"You can do it! Give it your all!"

Squeak! It was Thora! She was running along the shore waving a **miceking flag** at us. Was she really cheering us on?

My whiskers trembled with excitement. I stood up. "Oh, lovely Thora! I will give it my all, just for you!"

Thora continued. "You can do it, **BRAVE ONE!** Only you can turn that smarty-mouseking into a real hero!"

SHIVERING SQUIDS, Thora was only there to cheer for Max Musclepaw!

How heartbreaking!

Max had me row the ship, but it was a real **DISASTER**. I am not a sea-mouseking, so the drekar just kept **spinning** around and around!

Max Musclepaw shook his head.

"Forget the rowing!" he boomed. "Climb up the mast and **SET THE SAILS**!"

I obeyed, but my paws got **TANGLED** in the ropes. They *twisted* around me like strands of string cheese! At this rate, I would **NEVER** earn a miceking helmet!

Uh-oh!

THEA STILTONORD, GOAT WHISPERER!

The ship **SAILED** back to the port in Mouseborg. My sister, **THEA**, was waiting for us on the dock. Max explained that he had made an **agreement** with her for a special exercise.

"You'll all be riding **WILD HORSES**," Thea explained, and my fur froze in fear. Wild horses?!

"Geronimo, there are only four wild horses to work with, so I've got a very **special ride** planned for you," she told me as we walked.

"**S-S-SPECIAL?**" I stammered suspiciously.

Thea calmed me down. "Oh, don't worry. It's just a **friendly** goat!"

But as soon as I saw it, my knees became as *wobbly* as cottage cheese.

Great groaning glaciers!

It was the very same goat that had attacked me on Three Lookouts Cliff! I started to **RUN**, but Max grabbed me.

"Where do you think you're going, **shrimp**?" Max bellowed. "Behave like a true mouseking!"

He threw me into the pen with the **GOAT**, but that

Oh no, you again!

beast would not let me come near it! Then Thea came into the pen and WHISPERED some words to the goat to calm it down.

"Okay, Geronimo, climb on," she said.

And then she left me. Squeak!

1 The "friendly" goat began to **kick** and **huff**.

2 Then it **STOPPED** short and **THREW** me off its back!

3 I **spun** through the air . . . and landed in the boar pen!

That's when Sven the Shouter stomped up.
"Max, bring Geronimo to Gullet Valley
for his final test!"

Crusty codfish! Everyone knows that
Gullet Valley is very close to Beastgard, the
land of the fearsome dragons!

He doesn't
like me!

"Leave at once!" Sven yelled.
All the micekings shouted:

"SO SAYS SVEN THE SHOUTER!"

3

Um . . . hi!

WILD BEASTS IN THE WOODS

Max Musclepaw proudly announced his plans for our final test.

"TO COMBAT YOUR FEARS, YOU MUST FACE THEM!"

he boomed. "And what are micekings, even the bravest of us, afraid of? Dragons!"

I got CHILLS from the tips of my whiskers to the tip of my tail. I am not a brave mouseking at all!

"We will go look for the dragons!" Max continued. "We will **FACE** them! And we will DEFEAT them!"

"Face them? Face the dra . . . the dra . . .

the dra . . ."

I didn't finish my sentence because **I fainted from fright!**

When I opened my eyes, I saw a mouseking hovering over me.

"**WAKE UP**, you smarty-mouseking!" yelled Olaf the Fearless.

"Where am I?" I asked groggily.

"You're on the *Bated Breath*, of course!" he replied.

Squeak! I was headed for Gullet Valley, whether I liked it or not!

The ship sailed to the edge of a **tHICK FOrest**.

"These are the ELDERBERRY HONEY WOODS," Max told us. "They lead to Gullet

Valley. **MOVE IT ALONG!**"

We disembarked and marched through the **DARK TREES**. I swore I heard noises coming from behind the tree trunks.

"Trap, we're not **ALONE** in these woods!" I whispered.

"Don't be a 'fraidy mouse, Cousin!" Trap said.

This way!

I kept my ears open as we walked. I heard more strange sounds . . . **brushing** . . . **GRUMBLING** . . . **COMPLAINING** . . . Then I passed a tree trunk, and saw deep **CLAW MARKS** in it!

"Are there **w-w-wild beasts** in these woods?" I asked Max.

"Nope," replied Max. "Just some brown bears."

"**BROWN BEARS!** But they're wild beasts!" I cried.

"All they care about is **honey**," Max explained. "Just don't touch the **BEEHIVES** and you'll be fine."

I looked up. Dozens of beehives **dangled** from the tree branches overhead.

"With all these beehives, there must be a lot of bears," I said nervously.

I was thinking of all those bears with their **sharp claws** when I accidentally *tripped* over a big log in the path.

Crusher, Smasher, and Sprainer lifted the **LOG** and threw it like it was a little branch. When it hit the ground, however, **the whole forest floor shook**!

Out of the way!

Ouch!

plop!
plop!
plop!

Three beehives fell, breaking open as they hit the ground. GOLDEN HONEY spilled out of each one.

ROOOOAAAAR!!!

A chorus of threatening roars rose from the bushes.

I ran away with my paws in the air and my WHISKERS trembling in fright.

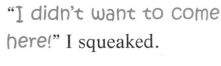

"I didn't want to come here!" I squeaked.

A Dragon's Tooth

I ran and ran as *FAST* as I could. It felt like my feet weren't even touching the ground. Had my **paws** sprouted wings?

"**Stop right there**, smarty-mouseking!" a voice bellowed.

It was Max Musclepaw. That's when I realized that I wasn't **flying**. The hero had lifted me up by my cloak. I was so **afraid** of the bears that I hadn't noticed!

"From now on, you will walk **BEHIND ME**, Geronimo," he said.

I nodded.

"And you will be *very quiet*, if you know what's good for you," Max continued. "Do you know what's **good** for you?"

"Yes," I squeaked.

He put me down and waved his arm at the scene in front of us. "We have reached **Gullet Valley**. This is the dragons' hunting ground. They **PROWL** the valley for miceking meat."

I gulped. **Squeak! I didn't want to be here.** I approached Max.

"What exactly is our final test?" I asked him.

"It's no big deal," he replied. **"You just have to pull out a dragon's tooth!"**

"A d-d-dragon's tooth?" I stammered.

Shivering squids, what an impossible task!

Suddenly, Max crouched down. "Hide, micekings! I hear a **NOISE** up ahead."

Trap snickered. "That's just the **chattering** of my scaredy-cousin's teeth."

"Not this time," Max said. He pointed. **"LOOK THERE!"**

We all peeked out from behind the bushes to see **two dragons** splashing around in a pool of **filthy** water!

"Let's get **closer**," Max whispered.

"Is that a good idea?" I asked. "Wouldn't it be smarter to get **far away**?"

But Max moved forward, followed by the others. Not wanting to be left alone, I followed.

What barbaric beasts!

"Thi**SSS** hot **SSS**pring **SSS**mell**SSS** of rotten egg**SSS**, Magmar," the green dragon was saying.

"Ye**SSS**, it'**SSS SSS**uperb!" agreed Magmar, the orange dragon. "But we should **SSS**peed thing**SSS** up, Rocky."

Magmar looked around. "If **Gobbler**

the Putrid knew we were relaxing in this
SSStinky pool in**SSS**tead of hunting for fresh
miceking meat, there would be trouble!"

Rocky snickered. "We
de**SSS**erve a little re**SSS**t!"

This is the life!

We shouldn't be here!

ROCKY

Rocky is a type of dragon known as a Rinser. He washes his miceking meat well before eating it.

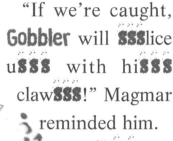

MAGMAR

Magmar is a young Slurper. He uses his long tongue to slurp up raw micekings — no ketchup necessary.

"If we're caught, **Gobbler** will **SSS**lice u**SSS** with hi**SSS** claw**SSS**!" Magmar reminded him.

"**SSS**tay calm," Rocky said. "Gobbler will never know. Now **relax**. We'll go back on patrol later."

Magmar rolled over in the pool, but he wasn't convinced.

Trap and I were **shivering** in fright. The other micekings didn't

scem afraid at all.

"What's the plan?" asked Crusher, Smasher, and Sprainer.

"Should we CRUSH them?"

"Should we SMASH them?"

"Should we SPRAIN their long tails?"

"Here's the plan," Max whispered. "I will go to the dragons and get their attention. The rest of you can SNEAK UP behind them."

"How will we get to their teeth if we are behind them?" I asked.

But Max ignored me and headed for the dragons. Crusher, Smasher, and Sprainer pushed me forward.

"Let's go, shrimp!" they said.

As we crept up behind the dragons, Max jumped out from behind a bush in front of them.

"Hey you two! You with the **ugly snouts**! I'm talking to you!" he taunted.

The two **DRAGONS** sat up and sniffed the air.

"Look at that mou**sss**eking over there!" Rocky said, spotting Max.

"*How lucky! A nice big one!*" said Magmar, licking his lips.

Max kept taunting them. "You big-nosed **blubberheads**! You lousy *lizards*! I will peel off your scales one by one!"

From our **HIDING** place we saw Rocky climb out of the pool. Crusty codfish! He was truly a **BIG** . . . no, **GIANT** . . . no, **ENORMOUSE** dragon!

How were we supposed to get one of

his teeth without being **chomped** and **SWALLOWED**?

I had no clue how to do it!

Once again I began to **shake** with fear. I was shaking so hard that I **bumped** into a pile of rocks behind me. The rocks **TUMBLED** to the ground, making a noise.

Magmar turned his head. "Look, more micekings**SSS**! This really i**SSS** our lucky day!"

The dragon moved toward us. "Which one shall I **SSS**lurp up fir**SSS**t?"

We were **FRIED**, **FINISHED**, **DONE FOR**!

Squeak! What could we do?

Suddenly, a huge **mud ball** hit Magmar square in the face.

"RUN! NOW!" yelled Max Musclepaw.

The brave mouseking pummeled Magmar and Rocky with mud balls. Trap dragged me away from the dragons.

"Let's get out of here, Geronimo! Quiiiiiiiick!"

MOUSEKING IN TROUBLE!

We ran as fast as we could. CRUSHER, SMASHER, and **SPRAINER** quickly charged ahead of us toward the woods. Trap and I followed them as they shouted back at us.

"THiS WAY!"
"BEHIND ME!"
"DOWN THIS PATH!"

I had no idea where we were going.

We kept ZIGZAGGING through the trees. It felt like we were going in circles.

"Where are we *running* to?" I called out.

Crusher, Smasher, and Sprainer looked at each other, confused, then each replied:

"THIS IS THE WAY!"

"TRUST US!"

"WE KNOW WHERE WE'RE GOING!"

So we kept following them until we ended up on the banks of a wild river.

"I don't remember this *river*," Crusher admitted.

"This doesn't look familiar," agreed Smasher.

"**WE'RE LOST!**" Sprainer yelled.

I sighed. I knew we were somewhere between the ELDERBERRY HONEY WOODS and Gullet Valley. There were two dragons behind us, and a river in front of us. We were **doomed**!

"**Good-bye**, miceking world!" I said dramatically. "FAREWELL, beautiful Thora!"

"Stop being such a blubberhead!"

Great groaning glaciers! That was the voice of Max Musclepaw. I looked up to see him standing on the other side of the river.

"Jump in the water and **SWIM** like herrings, all of you!" Max ordered. "The **DRAGONS** are coming!"

But the river was too big, and the **CURRENT** was too strong. If we tried to swim, we would be **swept away** by the roaring water.

I have a solution!

"I have a solution!" Trap exclaimed. "I am the village INVENTOR, aren't I?"

He quickly went to work, grabbing strong vines and tying them together end to end. When he finished, he had two **very long, very strong** vines.

I wasn't sure what Trap had in mind. Then he turned to Crusher.

"Toss one end of each over to Max," he instructed.

The three **beefy** micekings tossed the

ends of the two vines over to our leader. Then Trap yelled instructions over to Max.

Max *tied* the ends of the vines securely to a tree. Trap tied the other two ends to a **tree** on our side. The long vines **stretched** across the river.

I finally got it. Trap was making a *bridge*!

Crusher, Smasher, and Sprainer made their way over the SKINNY bridge like graceful tightrope walkers.

The bridge shook so much!

I, on the other paw, was **terrified**! I am afraid of heights, and I am not graceful! I am not an athletic mouseking — I am a scholar!

"CALM DOWN, Cousin. You'll make it," Trap said. "This bridge has been

Miceking Tested and Approved."

"Not by this mouseking!" I said. I **HUGGED** the tree. "I'm not going anywhere.

I'm staying here!"

"Fine!" Trap replied. "I'll cross first. But follow me, if you don't want to become **dragon food**."

He took a few steps onto the **swaying**, skinny bridge. **The bridge shook so much!**

Trap started to **wobble**. Then he slipped!

He slipped!

Oops!

Splaaash!

My cousin fell into the **freezing** waters of the river! His snout dipped under the water, and the **CURRENT** started to sweep him away! Max and the three beefy micekings just **STARED** at Trap, not sure what to do.

I had to do something. **BUT WHAT?**

Suddenly, my determination kicked in. I **QUICKLY** scrambled across the bridge, no longer afraid that I would fall in. (And I didn't!) Then I grabbed a vine **hanging** from a tree and threw it to my cousin.

"**Grab it, Trap!**" I yelled.

He grabbed the vine, and Crusher, Smasher, and Sprainer helped me **pull** Trap ashore.

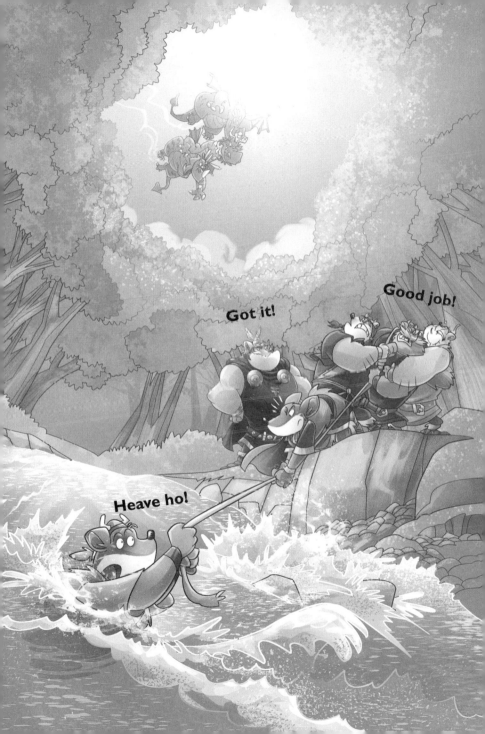

"Heeeeeave ho! Heeeeave ho!"
"Heeeeeave ho! Heeeeave ho!"
"Heeeeeave ho! Heeeeave ho!"

With one last tug, Trap fell at our feet.

"Thanks, Cousin. You **SAVED** me!" Trap exclaimed **happily**.

Max pounded me on the back. "Well done, shrimpy! You have made me **PROUD**."

Well done!

Thanks!

74

I couldn't believe my ears. The mouseking hero had given me a **compliment**! Maybe he would tell Sven the Shouter. And maybe, just maybe, I would finally earn a **MICEKING HELMET**!

I imagined myself wearing the helmet. Thora, beautiful Thora, would SMILE at me.

"Thora," I would say. "Will you — "

"Dragons!" Trap yelled, *jolting* me from my daydream.

Rocky and Magmar had found us!

NO MOUSEKING
LEFT BEHIND!

The two dragons **LUNGED** toward Max Musclepaw. Rocky grabbed his paws and Magmar grabbed his feet, and they **PULLED** on Max like he was taffy.

Magmar's stomach rumbled. He sniffed Max and blew his **stinky breath** in the mouseking's face.

"We caught you, you mou**SSS**eking troublemaker!" Magmar hissed. "You will be **SSS**uch a ta**SSS**ty **SSS**nack!"

He opened his jaws, ready to **gobble** up Max.

"**SSS**top!" roared Rocky. "That'**SSS** not how you do it!"

"What do you mean?" Magmar asked.

"You're **SSS**upposed to rin**SSS**e a mou**SSS**eking before eating him!" Rocky insisted.

Magmar shook his large head. "That'**SSS** not right! You'll wash off the flavor! *I want to eat him now!*"

"You don't know what you're **SSS**aying," Rocky argued. "I worked in the dragon **KITCHEN** with **SSS**izzle, Gobbler's cook. You mu**SSS**t rin**SSS**e before eating."

Magmar tried to distract him. "What about those other micekings? Did they e**SSS**cape?"

We hadn't. We were **HIDING** behind some trees, trying to decide what to do.

Rocky looked around. "They won't get far."

"**SSS**o let'**SSS** eat thi**SSS** one **NOW**, and then look for the other**SSS**," Magmar suggested.

"Fine!" growled Rocky, shooting FIRE from his nostrils. Then the two dragons flew off, carrying MAX with them.

"*Go back to the drekar without me!*" Max yelled bravely. What a hero! He was truly a fearless mouseking.

They got him!

Believe me, I wanted to **RUN**. But we couldn't leave Max in the **clutches** of those terrible dragons. I glanced at my companions.

Crusher, Smasher, and Sprainer are **BEEFY**, **bold**, and **courageous**, but without the guidance of Max Musclepaw they didn't know what to do. And Trap is good with inventions, but he's not exactly **brave**.

It was up to me, the **shrimpy** smarty-mouseking, to save the day.

"We will leave no mouseking behind!" I cried.

The other micekings nodded.

"I need your help," I said. "Together we can do this."

Crusher, Smasher, and Sprainer's eyes **lit up**.

"He's right! We'll CRUSH them!" said Crusher.

"We'll SMASH them!" said Smasher.

"We'll **SPRAIN** their tails!" said Sprainer.

Only Trap seemed unsure. "Okay, but how will we find the dragons?"

"Don't worry," I said. "I know what to do."

I had already come up with a mousetastic idea!

What an idea!

ON THE DRAGONS' TRAIL

I explained my plan, but my companions just **LOOKED** at me, confused.

"Are you sure it will work?" Trap asked.

My paws were **shaking** nervously as I replied, but I tried to sound confident. "Of course! If we climb up one of these trees, we will be able to see all of Gullet Valley. From there it will be easy to spot two **ENORMOUSE** dragons, and we can see where they're taking Max."

Crusher, Smasher, and Sprainer were not convinced.

"The **BARK** is too slippery!" said Crusher.

"The TREES are too tall!" said Smasher.

"We'll need a **really long** ladder," said Sprainer.

I thought about it. "We will be the ladder," I replied. "Each one of us can stand on the shoulders of the other. It's like I said: Together we can do this!"

Trap slapped me on the back with his paw. "Good idea, Cousin!"

"I'll be on the **BOTTOM**!" said Crusher.

Let's climb!

"And you can go on the t⊚p, Geronimo!" Trap said.

Only then did I understand the **TROUBLE** I had gotten myself into. My paws began to **shake** like a bowl of cheese curds.

"B-but . . . but I'm afraid of heights!" I stammered. "Can't one of **you** do it?"

"You're not making sense, Cousin," Trap replied. "You couldn't possibly hold up any of us with those **shrimpy** muscles of yours. You've got to climb to the top!"

I sighed. It was my plan, after all, so I couldn't back out. Besides, with each second that passed, Max Musclepaw was in **DANGER** of becoming dragon dinner!

Smasher climbed on Crusher's shoulders. Then Sprainer climbed on top of Smasher. Trap climbed on top of Sprainer. Then it was my turn.

I see them!

I slowly began to **climb**. I have never been good at **climbing** tall trees. I'm not good at **climbing** short ones, either!

One by one, I climbed up my companions.

"**Ouch!** You stepped on my ear!" cried Crusher.

"**Ouch!** Watch the whiskers!" cried Smasher.

"**Ouch!** No kicking!" cried Sprainer.

Finally, I stepped onto Trap's head and then climbed to the top of the tree.

Holey cheese, what a view!

A Sweet Plan

From the top of the tree I could see all of Gullet Valley, from the green Elderberry Honey Woods all the way to the BARREN land of the dragons.

"Can you see the dragons, Geronimo?" Trap yelled up to me.

I scanned the scene. Mostly, all I could see were the thick forest TREES. Then I spotted something: two balls of FIRE, followed by puffs of smoke. I yelled down to the others: "I see the dragons! They're in a clearing north of here!"

"Good job, Cousin! Come back down!" Trap yelled.

This excited the other three **micekings**,

who started to
pound the trunk
of the TREE with their
paws.

"We will CRUSH them!"

"We will SMASH
them!"

"We will SPRAIN
their tails!"

The tree began to shake!

I lost my grip and
slid down the trunk.

THUD! I landed
on my tail. Trap
helped me up.

I'm
sliiiiipping!

"Now how are we supposed to free Max Musclepaw?" he asked.

"**YES, HOW?**" echoed Crusher, Smasher, and Sprainer.

"I'm not sure yet," I replied. "Let's get a **CLOSER LOOK** at the situation."

I was deep in thought as we walked toward the clearing, and almost bumped into a **beehive**.

"Watch it, Cousin!" Trap warned. "You don't want to anger the **BROWN BEARS** again."

Crusty codfish, that was all we needed! Unless . . .

An idea hit me. Another **MOUSETASTIC** idea!

"Listen up, everyone," I told the others.

"We can use the brown bears to **CHASE AWAY** the dragons. We just have to make them believe that the dragons want to steal their **honey**!"

I pushed on a tree trunk, trying to get a beehive to **fall**.

But since I'm a **shrimpy** smarty-mouseking with PUNY muscles, I couldn't move the tree even half a tail.

LUCKILY, Crusher, Smasher, and Sprainer helped out.

I'm too weak!

Plop!
Plop!
Plop!

A dozen beehives fell to the ground. The sweet smell of honey spread through the woods.

A loud roar came from the bushes, and the big brown bears rushed out! They had

RRROOAAARRR

fierce claws and jaws filled with **sharp teeth**! We grabbed the beehives and ran away as **FAST** as we could.

THE CHARGE OF THE BROWN BEARS

When we reached the clearing, Rocky and Magmar were washing Max in a river along the ROCKY shore.

"How many timeSSS do we have to rinSSSe this mouSSSeking?" Magmar complained to Rocky. "I'm hungry!"

Rocky lifted up the soggy mouseking. "SSScrub under his pawSSS a bit more, Magmar! You'll SSSee how taSSSty he will be!"

"Wouldn't he be taSSStier with SSSome SSSeasoning?" Magmar argued. "Like maybe a SSSprinkle of hot pepper?"

"No, he would not," Rocky replied. "A

Put me down, you ugly lizards!

SCRUB SCRUB

fresh mouseking today is better than a **COOKED** one tomorrow!"

My whiskers **shivered** in fright when I heard those words. But I had a **MISSION** to complete! I couldn't turn back!

Then the dragons spotted us. "**LOOK**, Magmar! The micekings have returned!" Ricky cried.

"**SSS**weet!" hissed Magmar. "Now we can have de**SSS**ert!"

I gathered my courage. "Micekings, prepare to attack. Now!" I yelled in a trembling voice.

At that signal we all tossed our **BEEHiVES** at the two dragons. The hives **BURST** open, covering the dragons in **STiCKY** honey.

"I will gobble you all in one **sss**ingle bite!" Magmar roared, *lunging* toward us.

At that moment, the brown bears ran into the clearing. They were **BIG**, **hungry**, and . . .

SOOO SPEEEEEEDY!

Taken by **surprise**, Magmar and Rocky dropped Max. The mouseking quickly scurried off just as the bears jumped on the two dragons.

LICK! SLURP! GOBBLE!

The bears began to eat the honey that was stuck to the dragons.

"**OUCH!** These bear**sss** bite!" Rocky yelled.

"Get them off me!" wailed Magmar.

Trap taunted them. "Now you'll learn not to **mousenap** any of us, you **LOUSY LIZARDS**!" he called out.

Trap was lucky that the dragons couldn't chase him. They had too much **HONEY** stuck to their wings — and too many **bears** climbing on them!

The bears pushed the dragons back **one** step . . . **two** steps . . . **three** steps . . .

Rocky and Magmar fell into the river!

Everyone knows that dragons can't stand

clean water. It washes off their **terrible stench** (which is terrible to everyone but them). It also makes their scales squeaky, and can give them colds!

"Not freshwater!" Rocky wailed.

They yelled and blew SMOKE out of their dripping nostrils. But the water washed

Uh-oh!

I'm falling!

off the honey.

We watched them, satisfied, as they flew away.

MISSION ACCOMPLISHED!

Max Musclepaw **RAN** up to me.

"Looks like I made you into a **true macho mouseking**, didn't I, my shrimpy friend?" he asked.

I nodded and held out my paw. "Thanks!"

He shook it firmly. "I thought you were supposed to be a smarty-mouseking.

I am the one who should be thanking *you*. You saved me!"

Crusher, Smasher, and Sprainer lifted me above their heads.

Hooray!

Long live Geronimo!

"Hooray for Geronimo!"
Then they tossed me in the air and cheered:

"Hip, hip, hooray!"

"Hip, hip, hooray!"

"Hip, hip, hooray!"

"Hip, hip, hooray!"

I was so **touched** that I couldn't squeak!
Max looked like he might even CRY.
To hide his feelings, he THUNDERED,
"Back to the drekar! **True macho
micekings** never stop!"

My First Miceking Helmet!

The return trip went smoothly, and we arrived in **Mouseborg** at sunset. The whole village was waiting for us.

SVEN ran to meet us. "So, smarty-mouseking," he shouted, "did you manage to pull a **DRAGON'S TOOTH**?"

Great groaning glaciers, we had forgotten!

We were so worried about saving Max that we had forgotten about our *final test*!

"Well, you s-s-see —" I stammered, **afraid** to answer.

Max interrupted me.

"Valiant Sven, we did not finish the test,"

Max said. "Two dragons **captured** me."

Everyone gasped.

"Max Musclepaw was captured?" asked one mouseking.

"The hero who earned **1,753 helmets**?" asked another.

"How did he get free?" someone else asked.

Max motioned for everyone to be **silent**. "I'm free thanks to Geronimo. **He saved us all!**" he announced.

Sven patted me on the back. **"I'm proud of you!"**

It's about time!

My nephew **Benjamin** pushed through the crowd. He threw his arms around my neck.

"I knew you could do it, Uncle!" he cried.

THEA and **Trap** hugged me, too. And then, the charming **Thora** approached.

"You were so brave, Geronimo!" she said.

Shivering squids! Thora had just

called me **BRAVE**! I blushed from the tip of my tail to the tops of my ears.

"Umm, actually, I didn't really do anything S-S-SPECIAL," I stammered nervously.

Thora shook her head. "You behaved like a real hero, Geronimo, even without a miceking helmet!"

"That's right!" Max interrupted. "A feat like that should be **rewarded** with a miceking helmet!"

Sven nodded. "Micekings of Mouseborg, REJOICE! Geronimo will receive his first — and possibly last — **miceking helmet**!"

Everyone let out a celebratory cheer.

"LONG LIVE GERONIMO!"
"HOORAY FOR THE SMARTY-MOUSEKING!"
"WE'RE ALL WITH YOU!"

"We will celebrate with a lavish banquet!" Sven shouted. "And my wife, Mousehilde, will prepare gloog for the entire village!"

Mousehilde nodded. "I will make a huge pot of gloog! And when it's done, I'll make some MORE! And then some MORE . . . until you all tell me to stop!"

"Hooray! We love gloog!" yelled the villagers.

MOUSEHILDE headed toward her kitchen to make the gloog (an excellent stew, in case you're wondering). The other micekings ran to get ready for the feast. They put on their fanciest cloaks and curled their whiskers.

I couldn't move. I stood in the village square like a fly stuck in a bowl of cheese

soup. I was in shock. I was going to get my **FIRST** miceking helmet!

"*Geronimo, what are you still doing here?*" Thea asked me. "You can't go to the **feast** looking like this," she scolded. "You need to **wash** your fur and put on your best cloak!"

She had a point. After that incredible adventure with the dragons, I **stunk** worse than Stenchberg cheese.

So I **DRAGGED** myself home. I took a nice **hot bath** in the tub. Then I dried myself off and dragged myself

You need to go!

Where?

to the closet between yawns. I was so sleepy!

I was so tired — worn out — exhausted!

I had barely managed to put on some clean clothes when I collapsed on my bed and **passed out**!

A TRUE MOUSEKING
NEVER STOPS!

I was snoring deeply when I heard Thea's voice.

"**WAAAKE UUUP!** Geronimo, this is no time to sleep!"

I JUMPED out of bed. "Huh? What is it?" I yelled. "The dragons?"

Thea had her paws on her hips. "Really, Geronimo? There's a celebration in your honor and you're here snoring?"

"B-b-but I was just taking

Who? What? How?

a little rest," I tried to explain.

Thea **DRAGGED** me to the feast. Sven started **SHOUTING** as soon as he saw me.

"What happened to you, **smarty-mouseking**?" he asked.

"I'm s-s-sorry," I apologized. "I was so very, very tired."

"You were **tired**, eh?" Sven asked. "While all of us were **busy** preparing a feast in your honor? Is this how you thank us?"

Max Musclepaw stood up. "**Ten** laps around the Eternal Challenge Field!" the hero thundered. "Then **ONE HUNDRED** one-paw push-ups and **ONE THOUSAND** whisker lifts!"

"But . . . what about my **miceking helmet**?" I asked.

"No miceking helmet for you!" Sven

shouted. "That will teach you to fall asleep before your adventure is over. A **TRUE MACHO MOUSEKING** never stops!"

I wanted to **CRY**, but Thora approached me. "Don't worry, Geronimo. You'll have another chance to earn your helmet."

oh, lovely Thora! 💜 💜 💜

She was right. No matter how many times I had to try, I would earn my miceking helmet! I would do it!

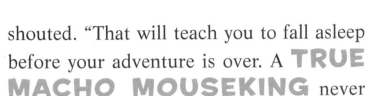

BUT THAT'S ANOTHER MICEKING STORY FOR ANOTHER DAY!

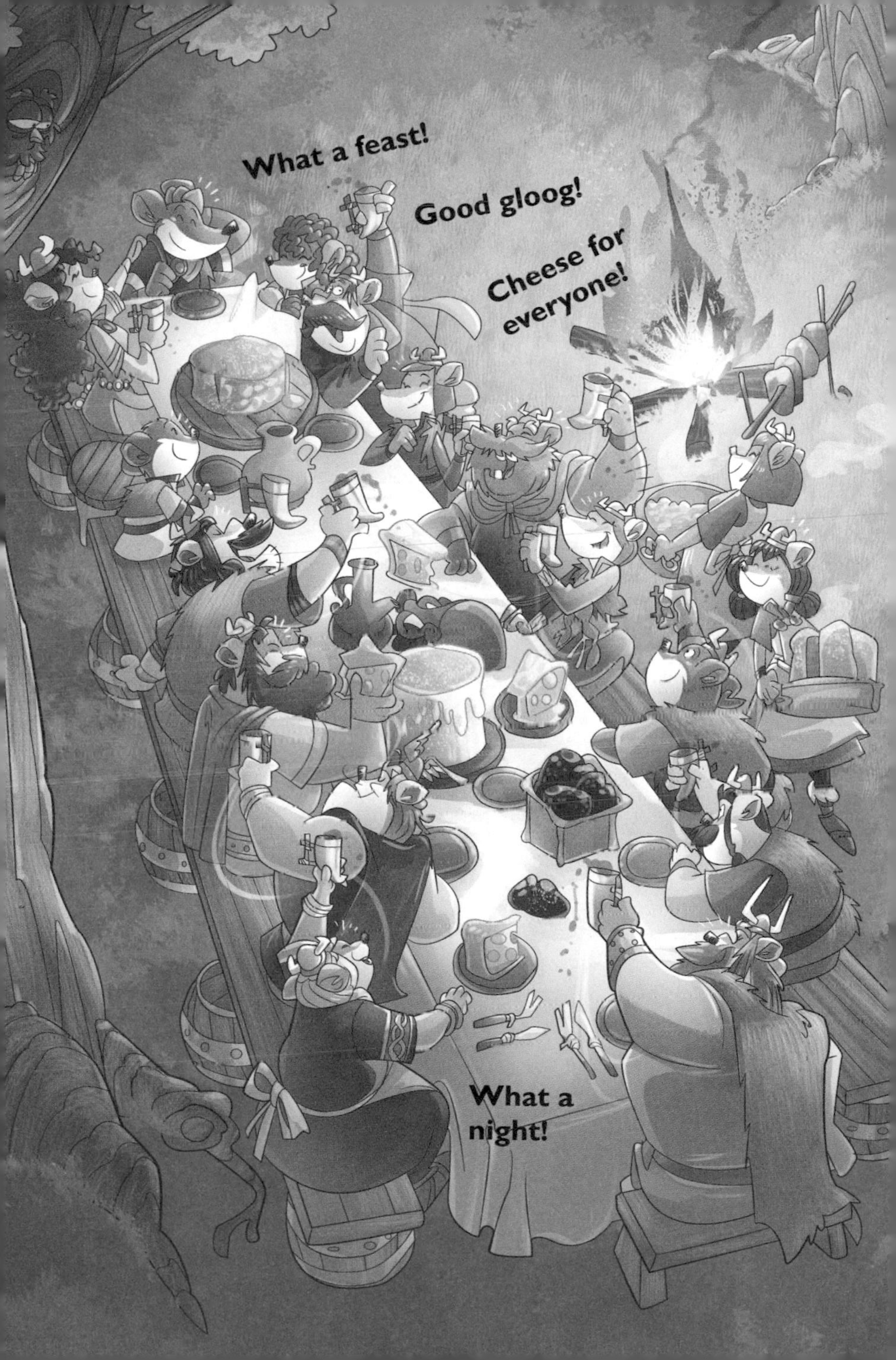
What a feast!
Good gloog!
Cheese for everyone!
What a night!

MICEKING ISLAND

Beastgard

Gullet Valley

Feargard

Forest of a
Thousand
Scales

Oofadale

Yawning
Cove

Helpful Hills

Mouseborg

Don't miss any adventures of the Micekings!

#1 Attack of the Dragons

#2 The Famouse Fjord Race

#3 Pull the Dragon's Tooth!

Up Next:

#4 Stay Strong, Geronimo!

Be sure to read all my fabumouse adventures!

#1 Lost Treasure of the Emerald Eye

#2 The Curse of the Cheese Pyramid

#3 Cat and Mouse in a Haunted House

#4 I'm Too Fond of My Fur!

#5 Four Mice Deep in the Jungle

#6 Paws Off, Cheddarface!

#7 Red Pizzas for a Blue Count

#8 Attack of the Bandit Cats

#9 A Fabumouse Vacation for Geronimo

#10 All Because of a Cup of Coffee

#11 It's Halloween, You 'Fraidy Mouse!

#12 Merry Christmas, Geronimo!

#13 The Phantom of the Subway

#14 The Temple of the Ruby of Fire

#15 The Mona Mousa Code

#16 A Cheese-Colored Camper

#17 Watch Your Whiskers, Stilton!

#18 Shipwreck on the Pirate Islands

#19 My Name Is Stilton, Geronimo Stilton

#20 Surf's Up, Geronimo!

#21 The Wild, Wild West

#22 The Secret of Cacklefur Castle

A Christmas Tale

 **#23 Valentine's Day Disaster**

 **#24 Field Trip to Niagara Falls**

 **#25 The Search for Sunken Treasure**

 **#26 The Mummy with No Name**

 **#27 The Christmas Toy Factory**

 **#28 Wedding Crasher**

 **#29 Down and Out Down Under**

 **#30 The Mouse Island Marathon**

 **#31 The Mysterious Cheese Thief**

 **Christmas Catastrophe**

 **#32 Valley of the Giant Skeletons**

 **#33 Geronimo and the Gold Medal Mystery**

 **#34 Geronimo Stilton, Secret Agent**

 **#35 A Very Merry Christmas**

 **#36 Geronimo's Valentine**

 **#37 The Race Across America**

 **#38 A Fabumouse School Adventure**

 **#39 Singing Sensation**

 **#40 The Karate Mouse**

 **#41 Mighty Mount Kilimanjaro**

 **#42 The Peculiar Pumpkin Thief**

 **#43 I'm Not a Supermouse!**

 **#44 The Giant Diamond Robbery**

 **#45 Save the White Whale!**

 **#46 The Haunted Castle**

 **#47 Run for the Hills, Geronimo!**

 **#48 The Mystery in Venice**

 **#49 The Way of the Samurai**

 **#50 This Hotel Is Haunted!**

 **#51 The Enormouse Pearl Heist**

 **#52 Mouse in Space!**

 **#53 Rumble in the Jungle**

 **#54 Get into Gear, Stilton!**

 **#55 The Golden Statue Plot**

 **#56 Flight of the Red Bandit**

 **The Hunt for the Golden Book**

 **#57 The Stinky Cheese Vacation**

 **#58 The Super Chef Contest**

 **#59 Welcome to Moldy Manor**

 **The Hunt for the Curious Cheese**

 **#60 The Treasure of Easter Island**

 **#61 Mouse House Hunter**

 **#62 Mouse Overboard!**

 **The Hunt for the Secret Papyrus**

 **#63 The Cheese Experiment**

 **#64 Magical Mission**

 **#65 Bollywood Burglary**

 **The Hunt for the Hundredth Key**

Don't miss any of my adventures in the Kingdom of Fantasy!

THE KINGDOM OF FANTASY

THE QUEST FOR PARADISE: THE RETURN TO THE KINGDOM OF FANTASY

THE AMAZING VOYAGE: THE THIRD ADVENTURE IN THE KINGDOM OF FANTASY

THE DRAGON PROPHECY: THE FOURTH ADVENTURE IN THE KINGDOM OF FANTASY

THE VOLCANO OF FIRE: THE FIFTH ADVENTURE IN THE KINGDOM OF FANTASY

THE SEARCH FOR TREASURE: THE SIXTH ADVENTURE IN THE KINGDOM OF FANTASY

THE ENCHANTED CHARMS: THE SEVENTH ADVENTURE IN THE KINGDOM OF FANTASY

THE PHOENIX OF DESTINY: AN EPIC KINGDOM OF FANTASY ADVENTURE

THE HOUR OF MAGIC: THE EIGHTH ADVENTURE IN THE KINGDOM OF FANTASY

THE WIZARD'S WAND: THE NINTH ADVENTURE IN THE KINGDOM OF FANTASY

Dear mouse friends,
thanks for reading,

and good-bye until
the next book!